The African Mask

Günter Gerngross

About this Book

For the Student

🎧 Listen to all of the story and do some activities on your Audio CD

🗨 Talk about the story

mail• When you see the green dot you can check the word in the glossary

K Prepare for Cambridge English: Key (KET) for Schools

For the Teacher

 A state-of-the-art interactive learning environment with 1000s of free online self-correcting activities for your chosen readers.

Go to our Readers Resource site for information on using readers and downloadable Resource Sheets, photocopiable Worksheets and Answer Keys. Plus free sample tracks from the story.

www.helblingreaders.com

For lots of great ideas on using Graded Readers consult Reading Matters, the Teacher's Guide to using Helbling Readers.

Level 2 Structures

Past simple of *be*	Comparative
Past simple	Comparative with *as...as*
Past simple (common irregular verbs)	Superlative
Be going to	*To* for purpose
Past Continuous	Adverbs of manner
Past simple v. past continuous	
	A lot of, not much, not many
Past simple in questions	*And, so, but, because*
Have to / Must	Possessive pronouns
Mustn't	

Structures from lower levels are also included

Contents

HELBLING DIGITAL

e·zone
THE EDUCATIONAL PLATFORM

HELBLING e-zone is an inspiring new state-of-the-art, easy-to-use interactive learning environment.

The online self-correcting activities include:

- reading comprehension;
- listening comprehension;
- vocabulary;
- grammar;
- exam preparation.

- ■ **TEACHERS** register free of charge to set up classes and assign individual and class homework sets. Results are provided automatically once the deadline has been reached and detailed reports on performance are available at a click.

- ■ **STUDENTS** test their language skills in a stimulating interactive environment. All activities can be attempted as many times as necessary and full results and feedback are given as soon as the deadline has been reached. Single student access is also available.

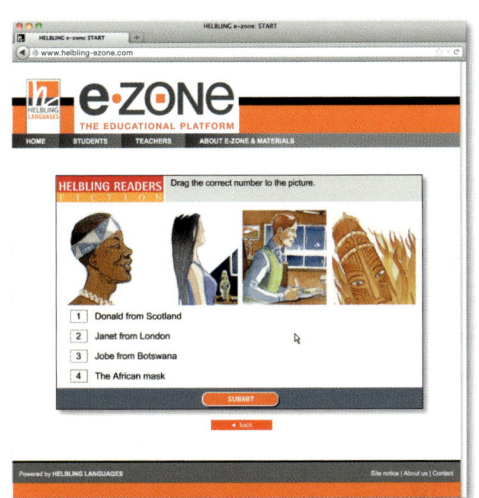

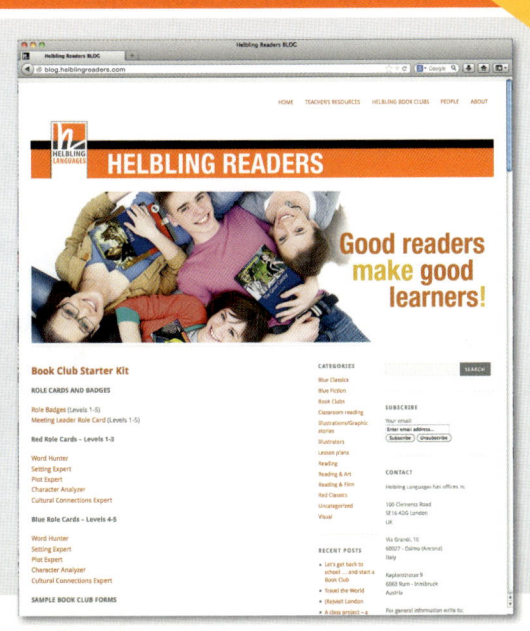

Before Reading

2 **1 The title of the book is *The African Mask*. What do you know about African masks? Listen and tick T (true) or F (false).**

	T	F
a) Children wear the masks.	☐	☐
b) The masks represent a spirit of a dead ancestor or an animal spirit.	☐	☐
c) The masks are plastic.	☐	☐
d) They make the paints from plants, trees and earth.	☐	☐
e) The colour black symbolizes death.	☐	☐
f) The masks are very special to their owners.	☐	☐
g) The masks protect the home.	☐	☐

2 In pairs, discuss the questions below.

- Do people make masks in your country?
- What are the masks made of?
- When and why do people wear them?

3 Look at the pictures in the book and guess the answers to the questions.

Where does the story take place?

a) ☐ Africa and Scotland

b) ☐ Africa and America

c) ☐ India and Scotland

d) ☐ America and India

What kind of story is it?

a) ☐ fantasy

b) ☐ detective

c) ☐ ghost story

d) ☐ science fiction

4 Describe the places in the pictures. Write 3 sentences about each one.

5 Which of the places above, would you most like to visit? Why? Tell the class.

When Janet came home from work on a hot day in August she picked up the mail●. "Bills●, bills, bills," she thought. Then she saw a blue envelope. She looked at the postmark●. "Who is writing to me from Scotland?" she wondered● and she opened the letter and started to read.

Dear Janet,
I hope you still live at the same address. This is Donald McKinnon. I hope you remember me and the brilliant time we had when we were skiing in Switzerland all those years ago. I often think of you and the time we spent together. I want to ask you a favour●. Can I invite you to come to my house in Scotland on the last weekend of September? I don't know how busy you are, but I really hope that you can come. Please write to me and let me know.
Love,
Donald

Janet put the letter on the table and sat down. Of course she remembered Donald and their holiday in Switzerland. They were in love and everything seemed perfect.

Glossary

- **bills:** letters to say you must pay something
- **favour:** thing you do to help someone
- **mail:** letters
- **postmark:** official mark on a letter that says where it comes from and when it is sent
- **wondered:** asked herself

After that holiday she moved to London to work and Donald stayed in Scotland. They wrote to each other for a while• but after a few months they broke up•.

"Donald McKinnon..." she thought. "I wonder what he's doing now."

Then she looked at her calendar. "The last weekend in September, why not?" she thought. "I'll send him an email straight away•." She checked the letter but there was no email address or phone number. So she sat down and wrote to Donald just like all those years ago...

- **broke up:** stopped being boyfriend and girlfriend
- **straight away:** immediately
- **while:** short period of time

Before she went to Scotland Janet bought a present for Donald. It was a small silver elephant. She got it in an African shop. Janet remembered• that Donald loved Africa. He always said that he wanted to go there one day.

She was excited• on Saturday as she went to the airport. She flew to Edinburgh and then she hired• a car at the airport when she arrived. The village where Donald lived was nearly an hour from the airport. When she arrived at the house the door was open but there was nobody there. There was a note• for Janet on the table in the hall. It said:

"Make yourself comfortable•. Your bedroom is the first room on the left upstairs. Dinner is at seven-thirty. See you then, D."

- **excited:** very happy and enthusiastic
- **hired:** paid money to use for a short period of time
- **make yourself comfortable:** relax
- **note:** short letter
- **remembered:** recalled; thought of something again

Janet left her things in her room and then she went out for a walk. The village was small but it was full of people. There was a market in the square and the farmers were buying and selling their sheep. Janet went for a coffee. When she was leaving the café it was raining. A man offered to share• his umbrella with her. But when she said she was going to Donald McKinnon's house he excused himself• and hurried away•. Janet walked home in the rain. "What's wrong with Donald's house?" she wondered.

- **excused himself:** made an excuse and left
- **hurried away:** went away in a hurry
- **share:** (here) use together

Back at Donald's house she had a shower and changed her clothes. It was nearly time for dinner and she was looking forward to● seeing Donald again.

When she went downstairs he was waiting for her. He gave her a big hug● and thanked her for coming. Janet looked at Donald. There was something different about him but she couldn't work out● what it was. Janet suddenly thought: "I know – Donald is very sad."

● **hug:** when you put your arms around someone
● **looking forward to:** happy about something in the future

● **work out:** solve (a problem); think

They went into the dining room. The table was set● and full of lovely food. As they ate Janet talked about London, her friends and her work. Donald just talked about their holiday in Switzerland. "Those were the best days of my life," he said. When she asked him about his life now Donald didn't speak for a long time. Then he told her that he lived in Africa for five years.

"There is one thing I must tell you," he said. "I had a friend in Botswana called Jobe Musowe and he often invited me to his house. There was a beautiful wooden mask in his living room. The mask was very important to Jobe's family. He said it brought them luck.
I loved the mask and I really wanted to have it. But of course I couldn't ask my friend to sell it to me." Donald stopped. He was very white in the face.

After a while Donald went on. "One day I took a photo of the mask and I gave it to a man who made wooden masks. I asked him to make a copy of the mask in the photo. When it was finished my mask looked the same as the mask in Jobe's house. But I was still not happy. I needed the one in my friend's house. One day I knew Jobe was away so I took my mask to his house and swapped● it with the one on the wall.

Soon after that I left Africa. I did not hear from Jobe for a long time. Then one day I got a letter. He was very ill●. The doctors could not help him. When his wife called a medicine man● from one of the villages the man told him to burn the mask.
Jobe didn't want to do that, but when he looked very closely at the mask he saw that it was not the original● one. So he burned the new mask and immediately he got better." Donald stopped. He looked very tired.

"I don't feel well," said Donald. "And you must be tired after your journey. Thank you again for coming, Janet."
Then he said good night and they went upstairs to their bedrooms.

That night Janet had a very bad dream. In her dream she saw an African mask that looked like Donald. The mask could speak, but Janet didn't understand what it was saying. Then somebody threw the mask into a fire. Janet wanted to save it, but it was too late.

When Janet came down in the morning the dishes• from the night before were cleared•. There was breakfast on the table, but there was no sign of Donald•. She called his name, but there was no answer. "Maybe he has gone into the village," thought Janet.

An hour later there was a knock at the door. Janet opened it and there was a man outside.

"Hello, I'm Fergus McClennan," he said. "I'm Donald McKinnon's solicitor•."

"Donald's not here at the moment," said Janet. The solicitor looked at her and then he said, "I know, Donald died two weeks ago. He asked me to come here today and tell you that this house is now yours. Can you sign these papers?"

Glossary

- **cleared:** taken from the table
- **dishes:** plates, etc.
- **solicitor:** legal person
- **there was no sign of Donald:** Donald was not there

19

Janet was completely confused. "Was I dreaming yesterday?" she thought.

Then she remembered the man with the umbrella and how he hurried away when she said Donald's name.

She didn't tell the solicitor about her dinner with Donald the night before. She signed the papers and then she looked through the house. She found the African mask hanging on the wall in Donald's study. Suddenly Janet felt very scared. She left the room and locked● the door. Then she packed● her things, locked the house, drove to the airport and flew home.

The next day she went to see her best friend Anna. She told Anna about her dinner with Donald and that Donald was dead and she was now the owner● of the house. Janet also told her about the African mask.

"It's a beautiful house," she said, "but I'm scared of the mask and I don't want to go there on my own. Can you come to Scotland with me next weekend?" she asked her friend.

"Of course, I can," said Anna.

● **owner:** person who has something; who something belongs to

When Janet unlocked● the door of her house in Scotland the following weekend everything seemed to be fine●. The two friends went for a walk, had coffee, bought some food, and then went back to the house to make dinner.

After dinner Janet decided to show her friend the mask in Donald's study. But when she opened the door the mask was not on the wall but on the chair in front of Donald's desk.

"Maybe you took it off the wall and put it on the chair," Anna said. Janet was scared. That night both Janet and Anna heard somebody crying. They switched on● the lights but there was nobody there. And when they went into the study the next morning the mask was on the floor.

Anna said: "I think there's a ghost● in the house. And I think you must give the mask back to its owner. Let's check● Donald's desk and see if we can find an address for his friend in Africa." They went into the study and after a while they found a letter from Jobe Musowe to Donald.

They also found an envelope with Janet's name on it and a large sum● of money inside.

Janet and Anna carefully put the mask in a box and went back to London.

Janet asked for time off● work. She also wrote to Jobe Musowe saying that she had something to give him from Donald.

Glossary

- **check:** (here) look in
- **fine:** okay
- **ghost:** spirit of a dead person
- **sum:** quantity
- **switched on:** turned on (light or other electrical thing)
- **time off:** holidays from
- **unlocked:** opened with a key

Two weeks later she flew to Botswana and went straight from the airport to Donald's friend's house.

Jobe Musowe was very surprised when Janet told him her story.

He and his wife invited Janet for dinner and when she took the mask out of the box they were both very happy. They put it back in its old place. Janet felt that the mask was at peace now.

The next day she flew back to London, and the following weekend she went with Anna to the house in Scotland once more.

When they arrived the window of Donald's study was open, and that night there was no ghost and no crying.

"Donald is at peace, too," thought Janet.

And she smiled.

After Reading

1 Who says or thinks this? Match the characters with the speech bubbles.

a)  b)

c) d)

1 I know, Donald died two weeks ago.

2 Those were the best days of my life.

3 I think there's a ghost in the house.

4 What's wrong with Donald's house?

2 Complete the sentences with the characters' names.

Donald (x2)	Janet	Anna	Jobe

a) .... went on a skiing holiday with Donald many years ago.

b) .... lived in Africa for five years.

c) .... 's house is in a little village in Scotland.

d) ....'s family believed that the beautiful wooden mask brought them luck.

e) .... told Janet to take the mask back to Africa.

K **3** Complete the sentences about the mask with the past simple of the verbs below.

make	see	burn	get
die	tell	want	go
believe	bring	steal	

a) Donald saw the mask in Jobe's living room and he .... it.

b) Jobe .... that the mask .... his family luck.

c) A man .... a copy of the mask for Donald.

d) Donald still wanted Jobe's mask so one day he .... it.

e) Donald .... back to Scotland with the mask.

f) Jobe got very ill. The medicine man .... him to burn the mask.

g) Jobe .... that it was not the original mask so he .... it.

h) Jobe immediately .... better but Donald .... soon after.

4 In pairs, discuss.

Can masks have special powers?
Why did Donald die?
Janet took the mask back to Africa. Did she do the right thing?

5 Are you superstitious? Do you have a good luck charm? Do a class survey and find out the things people keep to bring them luck.

Are you superstitious?

Do you have a good luck charm?

After Reading

1 What is happening? Look at the pictures and write sentences.

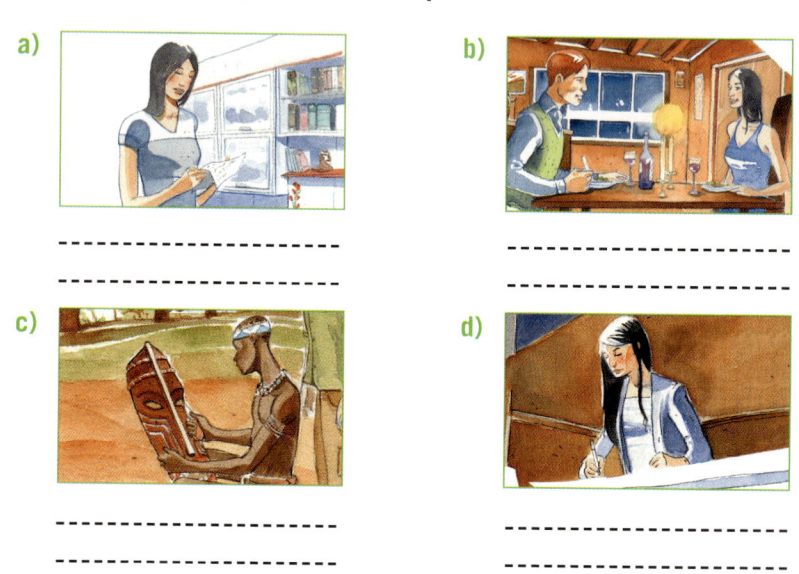

a)

----

b)

----

c)

----

d)

----

2 Much of the story is set in Scotland. What do you know about Scotland? Do the quiz below.

a) What is the capital of Scotland?

1 ☐ Glasgow

2 ☐ Aberdeen

3 ☐ Edinburgh

b) Who is 'Nessie'?

1 ☐ A Scottish princess

2 ☐ A legendary monster

3 ☐ A famous pop group

c) What is tartan?

1 ☐ A special cloth that each Scottish family has

2 ☐ A meal served at Halloween

3 ☐ A festival of Scottish dancing and music

3 **Read the text about African medicine men.**

The Medicine Men of Africa

Some people in rural Africa still have strong beliefs in supernatural powers. And you can still visit a medicine man or a witch doctor. Some medicine men say they have supernatural powers and they can heal people with magic. Some medicine men use the roots, bark and leaves of plants and trees to heal people.

A French doctor watched a medicine man in the Congo close a deep cut in a man's arm. He didn't use a needle and thread. He used ants. In Dakar, in Senegal, a medicine man saved the lives of a lot of patients with yellow fever. The hospital doctors couldn't do anything for them.

4 **Tick (✓) true (T) or false (F) below.**

	T	F
a) People in Africa don't believe in supernatural powers.	☐	☐
b) Some medicine men use plants.	☐	☐
c) All medicine men use magic.	☐	☐
d) The hospital doctors couldn't save the patients with yellow fever.	☐	☐
e) A medicine man in Senegal used magic to close a cut.	☐	☐

5 **Use the Internet and find out about medicine men in Africa. Then tell the class.**

After Reading

1 Circle the correct words to complete the summary of the story.

One day, Janet received **(a) an email / a letter** from Scotland. It was from an old friend, Donald. Donald invited Janet to come to Scotland to visit him. Janet accepted his invitation and a few weeks later, she **(b) flew / drove** to Scotland. When she arrived at Donald's house, there was **(c) a lot of people / nobody** there. She went for a coffee in the village.

That evening, when she went downstairs, Donald was there. He was very happy to see Janet but he looked **(d) frightened / sad**. He told Janet about his life in **(e) Africa / India**. "I stole a wooden mask from my friend, Jobe, and I brought it to Scotland. The mask was **(f) very / not very** important to my friend," he said. "Later I got a letter saying that Jobe was very **(g) happy / ill**. He went to a medicine man. The medicine man told him to **(h) swap / burn** the mask. Jobe burnt the mask and then he felt **(i) better / worse**."

The next morning, Janet went downstairs. The house was empty. An hour later a **(j) farmer / solicitor** came. "Donald died two **(k) weeks / years** ago," he told Janet. "This house is yours. He wanted you to have it." Later Janet saw the mask on the wall. She felt **(l) sad / scared** and left the house.

The next weekend, Janet went to the house with her friend Anna. That night they both heard someone **(m) crying / laughing**. Anna said, "I think there is a **(n) thief / ghost** in the house. You must give back the mask." So Janet took the mask back to Africa. Donald's friend Jobe was very **(o) happy / frightened** to see the mask. The next time Janet went to Scotland, there was no ghost and no crying in the night. The mask was **(p) burned / at peace**.

2 Do you know any ghost stories? Write the story. Then tell it to a friend.

3 Read the text about Botswana and then complete the fact file below.

Botswana is in Southern Africa. It became an independent country in 1966 and it has a population of over one and a half million people. Its capital is Gabarone and the official languages are English and Tswana.

It is mostly flat with some mountainous areas. It has a semi-arid climate, with warm winters and hot summers.

The Kalahari desert covers most of the south of Botswana. Its name means 'place without water' in the Tswana language. You can see lions, hyenas and meerkats there.

There are grasslands in the North of the country. Many people travel to Botswana to see the wildlife. They go to the Okavanga Delta, which is the world's largest inland delta. And it is home to lots of wild animals such as elephants, crocodiles, wildebeest, hippopotamuses, giraffes and cheetahs.

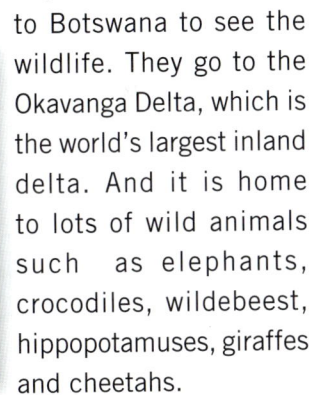

Name: ....

Population: ....

Capital: ....

Climate: ....

Geography: ....

Animals: ....

4 Donald was interested in Africa. He always wanted to go there. Where do you want to go? Look on the Internet and then write a fact file of the country.

Stick a picture here

Name: ....

Population: ....

Climate: ....

Geography: ....

Animals: ....

After Reading

PUZZLE

1 Can you remember these words? Read the clues and complete the puzzle with words from the story.

a) Donald ....the two masks and he took Jobe's mask.

b) Janet looked at the .... on the letter. Then she knew the letter was from Scotland.

c) Janet goes to Scotland for the first time on the last weekend in ....

d) Donald wrote and asked Janet to do him a ....

e) Jobe believed that the mask brought his family good ....

f) At the airport in Edinburgh, Janet .... a car and then drove to Donald's village.

g) Janet bought a silver elephant as a .... for Donald.

h) Donald gave Janet a .... when he saw her.

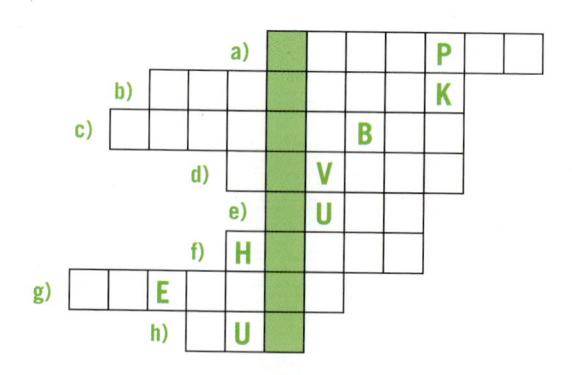

2 There is a mystery word in the puzzle. Complete the sentence below with the mystery word.

.... the mask brought Donald bad luck.